D1217907

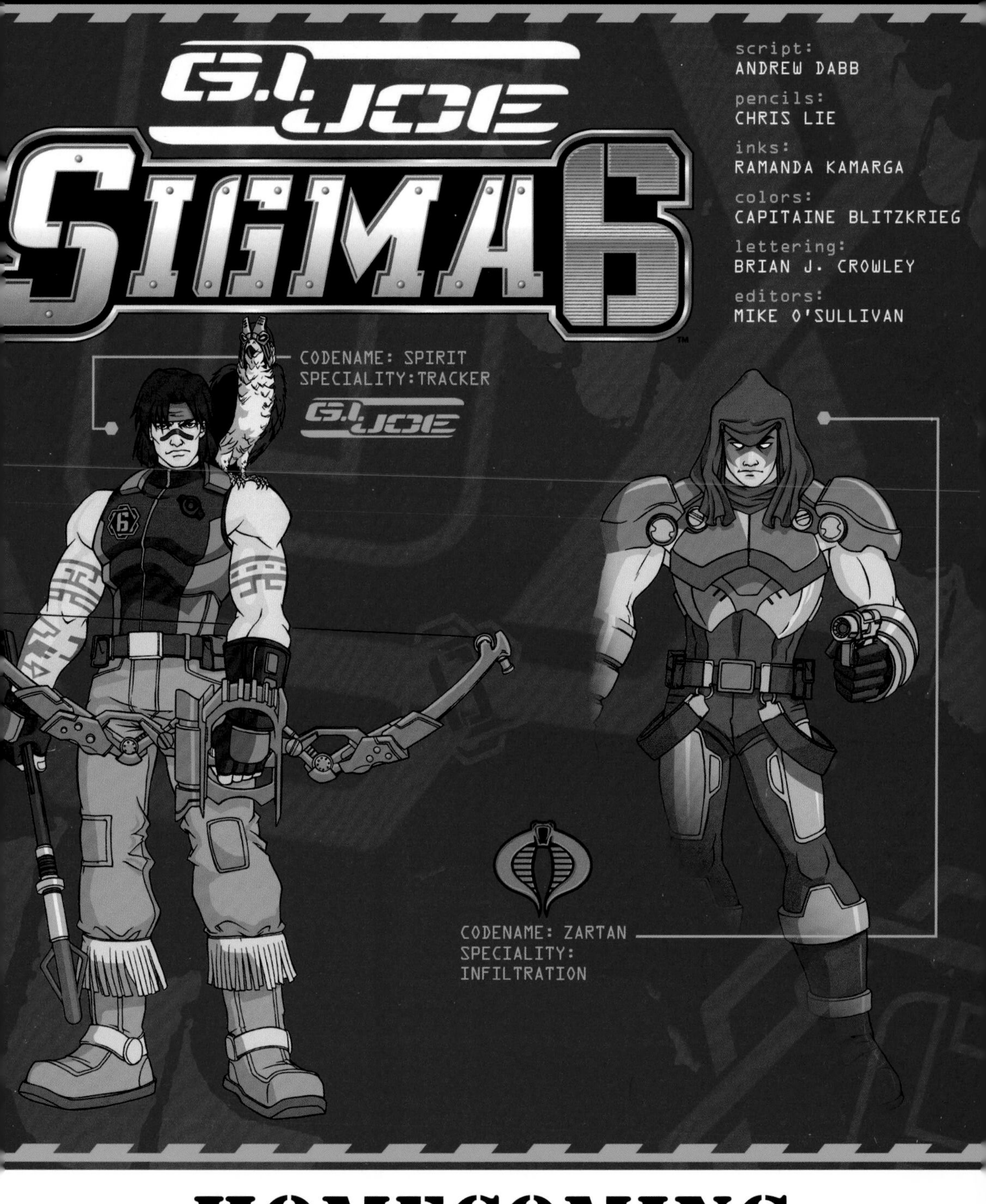
G.I. JOE
SIGMA 6™
script:
ANDREW DABB
pencils:
CHRIS LIE
inks:
RAMANDA KAMARGA
colors:
CAPITAINE BLITZKRIEG
lettering:
BRIAN J. CROWLEY
editors:
MIKE O'SULLIVAN
CODENAME: SPIRIT
SPECIALITY:TRACKER
G.I. JOE
CODENAME: ZARTAN
SPECIALITY:
INFILTRATION

HOMECOMING

visit us at www.abdopublishing.com

Exclusive reinforced library bound edition published in 2008 by Spotlight, a division of ABDO Publishing Group, Edina, Minnesota. This edition is produced under agreement with Devils Due Publishing, Inc. www.devilsdue.net

Library of Congress Cataloging-in-Publication Data

Dabb, Andrew.
   Homecoming / script, Andrew Dabb ; pencils, Chris Lie ; inks, Ramanda Kamarga ; colors, Capitaine Blitzkrieg ; lettering, Brian J. Crowley ; editor, Mike O'Sullivan. -- Exclusive reinforced library bound ed.
      p. cm. -- (G.I. Joe SIGMA 6)
   Revision of issue 2 (Jan. 2006) of G.I. Joe Sigma 6.
   ISBN-13: 978-1-59961-372-7
   ISBN-10: 1-59961-372-7
   1. Graphic novels. I. Lie, Chris. II. O'Sullivan, Mike. III. G.I. Joe SIGMA 6. 2. IV. Title.

PN6727.D23H66 2008
741.5'973--dc22

                                    2006052225

All Spotlight books have reinforced library bindings
and are manufactured in the United States of America.

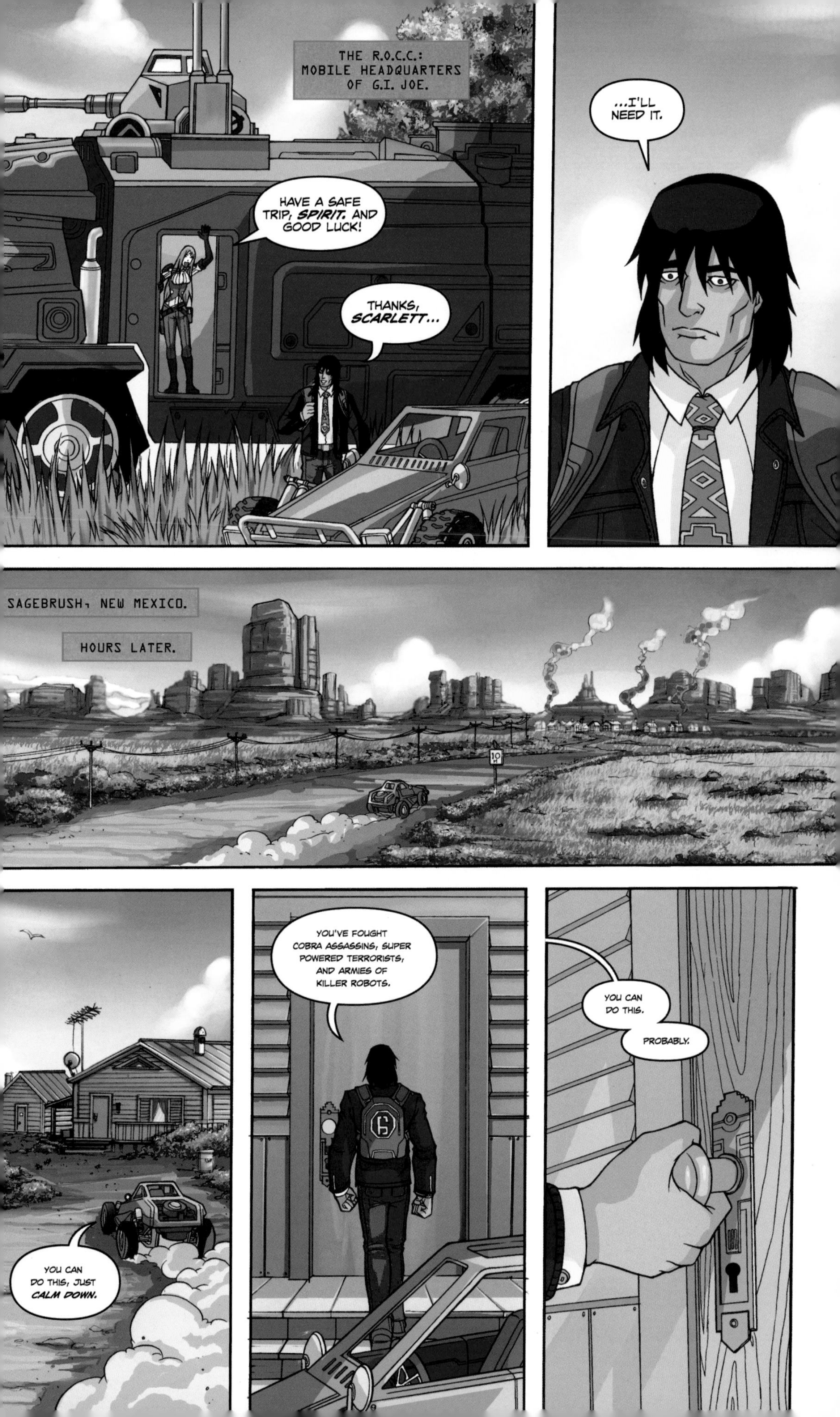
THE R.O.C.C.: MOBILE HEADQUARTERS OF G.I. JOE.
HAVE A SAFE TRIP, SPIRIT. AND GOOD LUCK!
THANKS, SCARLETT...
...I'LL NEED IT.
SAGEBRUSH, NEW MEXICO.
HOURS LATER.
10
YOU CAN DO THIS, JUST CALM DOWN.
YOU'VE FOUGHT COBRA ASSASSINS, SUPER POWERED TERRORISTS, AND ARMIES OF KILLER ROBOTS.
YOU CAN DO THIS.
PROBABLY.

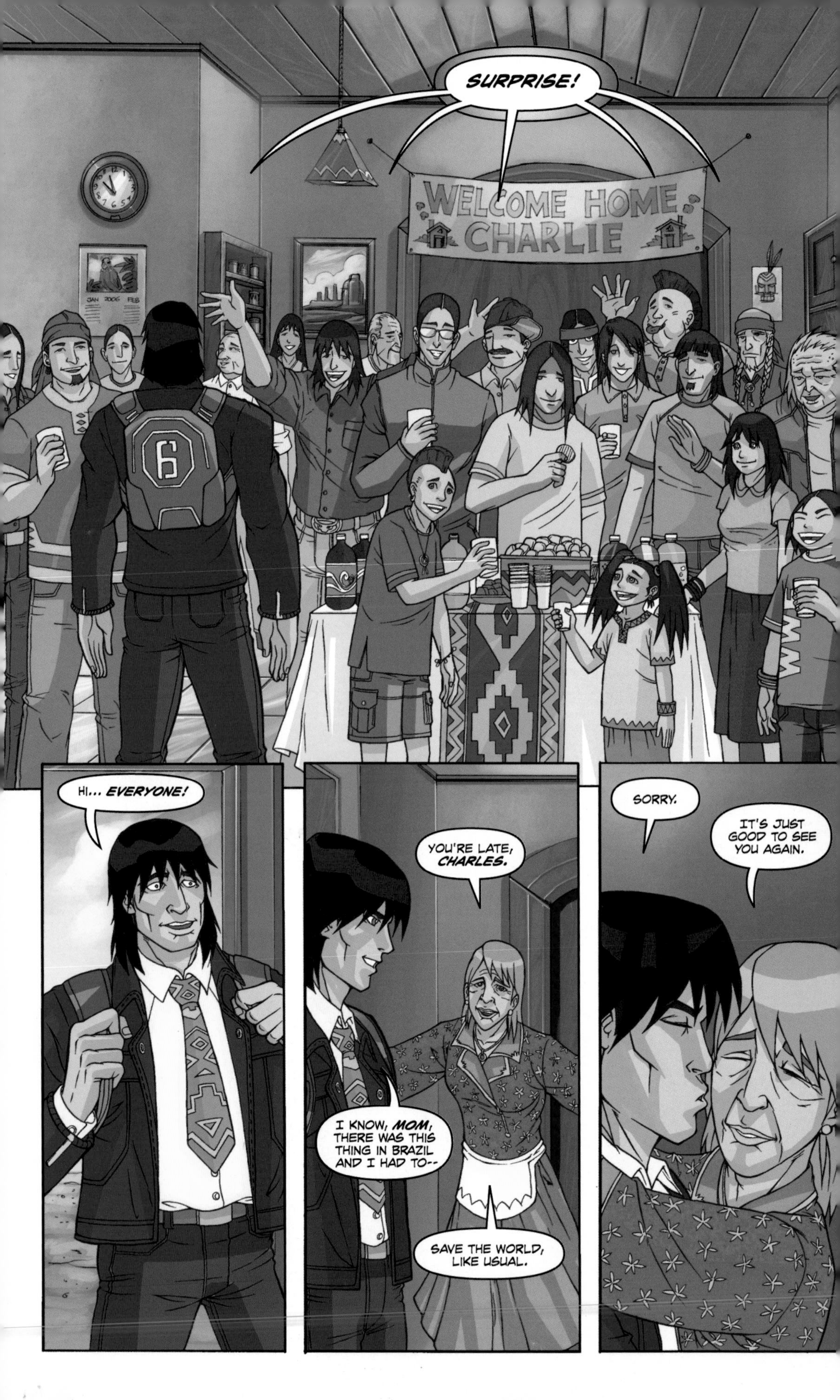
SURPRISE!
WELCOME HOME CHARLIE
JAN 2006 FEB
HI... EVERYONE!
YOU'RE LATE, CHARLES.
I KNOW, MOM, THERE WAS THIS THING IN BRAZIL AND I HAD TO--
SAVE THE WORLD, LIKE USUAL.
SORRY.
IT'S JUST GOOD TO SEE YOU AGAIN.

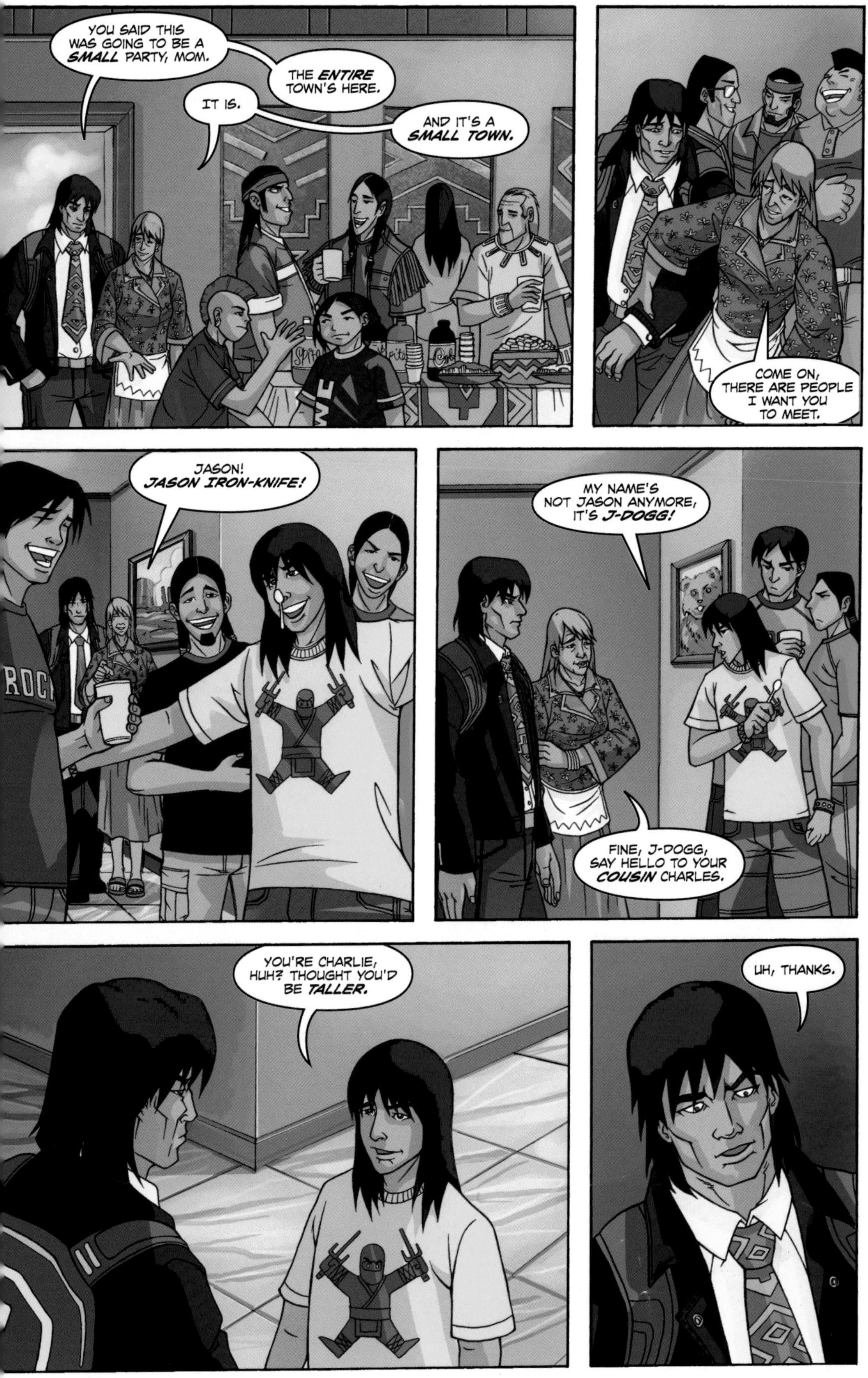
YOU SAID THIS WAS GOING TO BE A SMALL PARTY, MOM.
THE ENTIRE TOWN'S HERE.
IT IS.
AND IT'S A SMALL TOWN.
COME ON, THERE ARE PEOPLE I WANT YOU TO MEET.
JASON! JASON IRON-KNIFE!
MY NAME'S NOT JASON ANYMORE, IT'S J-DOGG!
FINE, J-DOGG, SAY HELLO TO YOUR COUSIN CHARLES.
YOU'RE CHARLIE, HUH? THOUGHT YOU'D BE TALLER.
UH, THANKS.

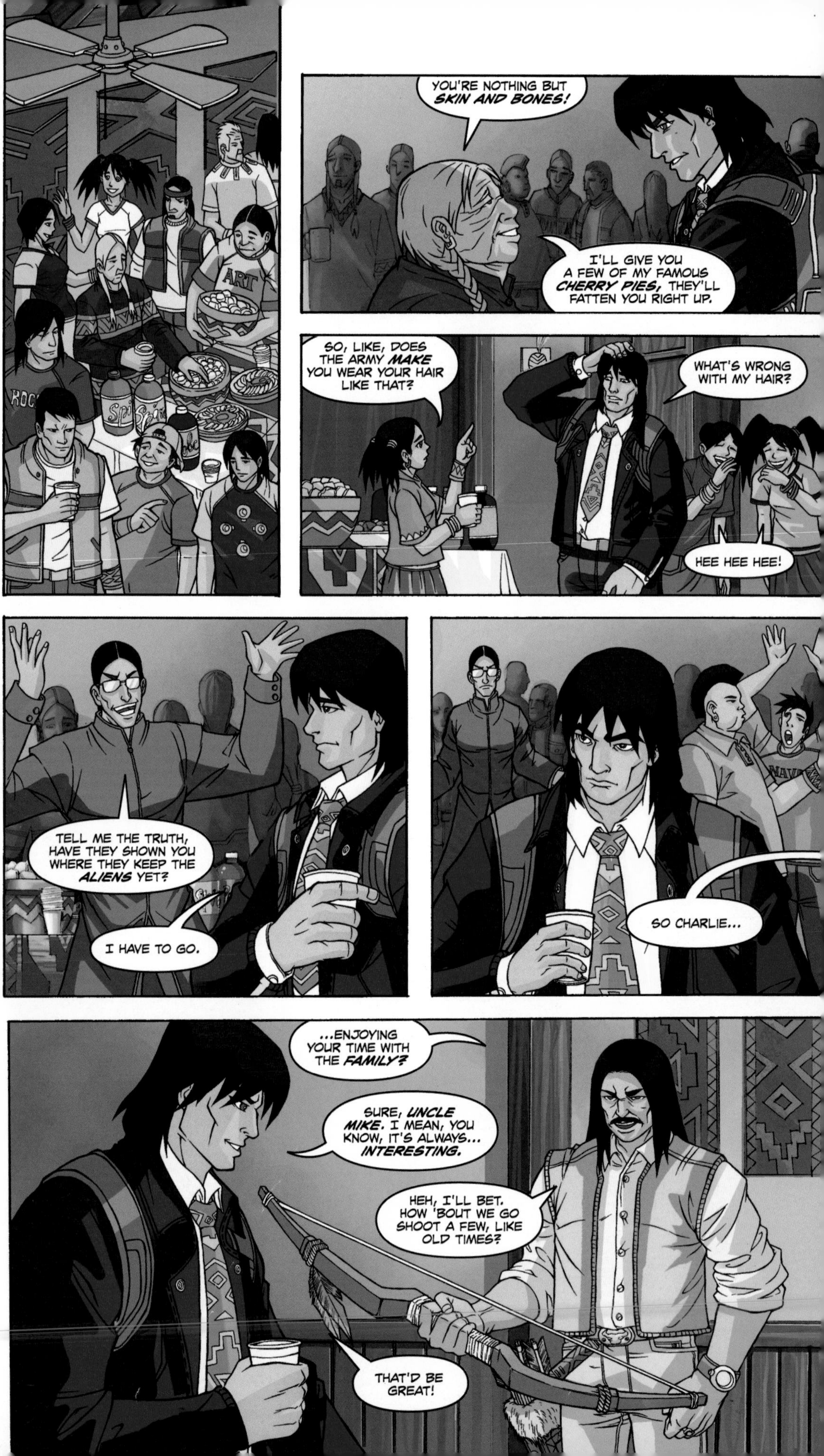
YOU'RE NOTHING BUT SKIN AND BONES!
I'LL GIVE YOU A FEW OF MY FAMOUS CHERRY PIES, THEY'LL FATTEN YOU RIGHT UP.
SO, LIKE, DOES THE ARMY MAKE YOU WEAR YOUR HAIR LIKE THAT?
WHAT'S WRONG WITH MY HAIR?
HEE HEE HEE!
TELL ME THE TRUTH, HAVE THEY SHOWN YOU WHERE THEY KEEP THE ALIENS YET?
I HAVE TO GO.
SO CHARLIE...
...ENJOYING YOUR TIME WITH THE FAMILY?
SURE, UNCLE MIKE. I MEAN, YOU KNOW, IT'S ALWAYS... INTERESTING.
HEH, I'LL BET. HOW 'BOUT WE GO SHOOT A FEW, LIKE OLD TIMES?
THAT'D BE GREAT!

BZAP

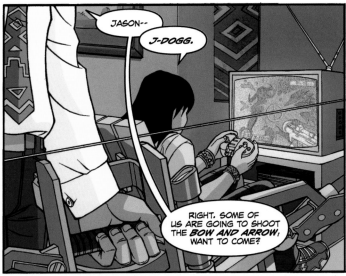

JASON--

J-DOGG.

RIGHT. SOME OF US ARE GOING TO SHOOT THE *BOW AND ARROW*, WANT TO COME?

A BOW AND ARROW? SERIOUSLY?

WHAT?

IT'S A LITTLE LAME, DON'T YOU THINK?

ZZAK

NO, I DON'T. THESE WEAPONS HAVE BEEN PART OF *NAVAJO CULTURE* FOR HUNDREDS OF YEARS--

YEAH, YEAH. ANCESTORS, HERITAGE, TRADITION, WHATEVER.

LISTEN, CHUCK, YOU STICK WITH YOUR BOW AND ARROW, I'LL STICK WITH MY PLASMA DEATH RAY, AND WE'LL BOTH BE HAPPY, OKAY?

BZAP

SUIT YOURSELF.

SPLORCH

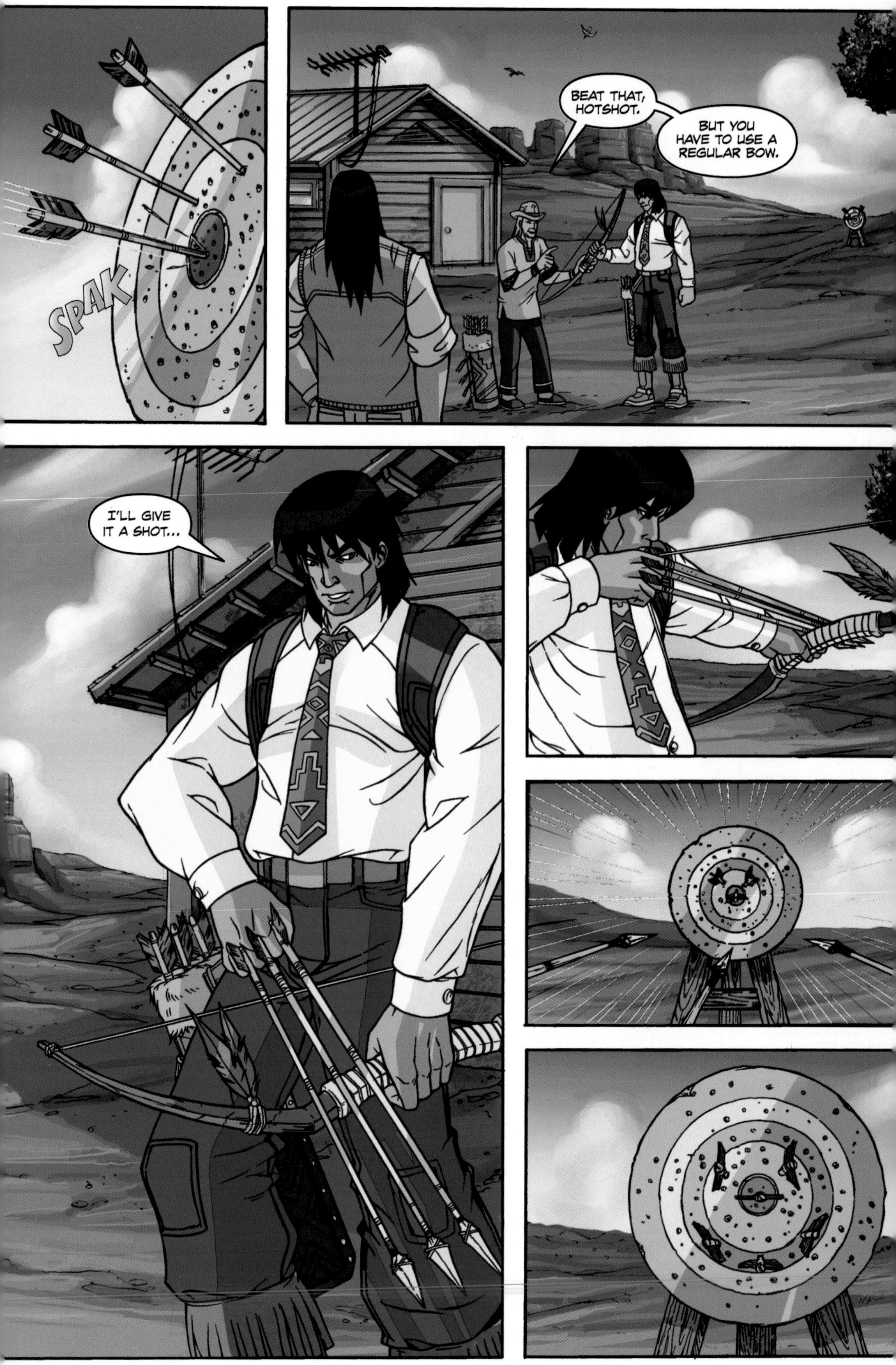
SPAK
BEAT THAT, HOTSHOT.
BUT YOU HAVE TO USE A REGULAR BOW.
I'LL GIVE IT A SHOT...

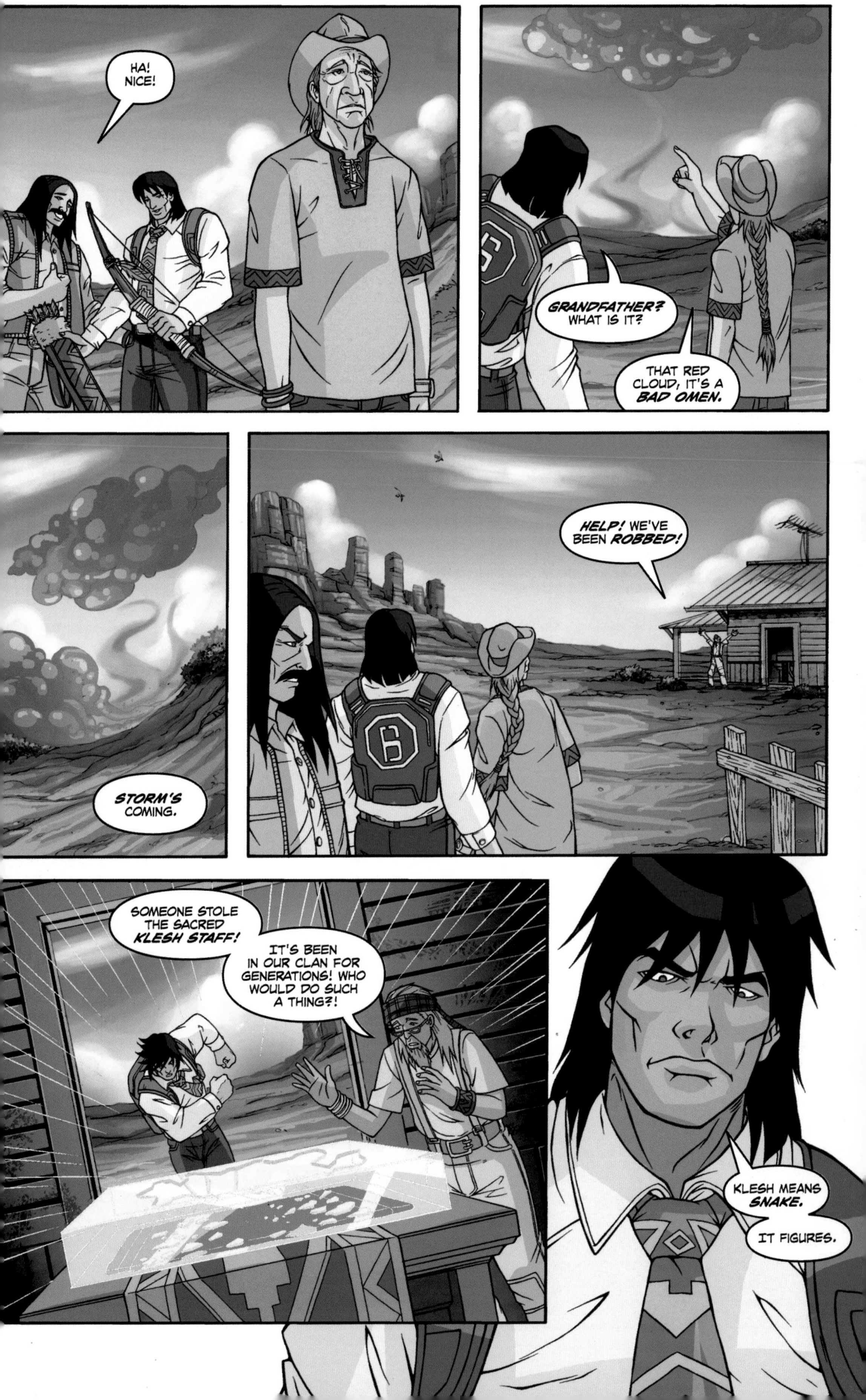
HA! NICE!
GRANDFATHER? WHAT IS IT?
THAT RED CLOUD, IT'S A BAD OMEN.
STORM'S COMING.
HELP! WE'VE BEEN ROBBED!
SOMEONE STOLE THE SACRED KLESH STAFF!
IT'S BEEN IN OUR CLAN FOR GENERATIONS! WHO WOULD DO SUCH A THING?!
KLESH MEANS SNAKE.
IT FIGURES.

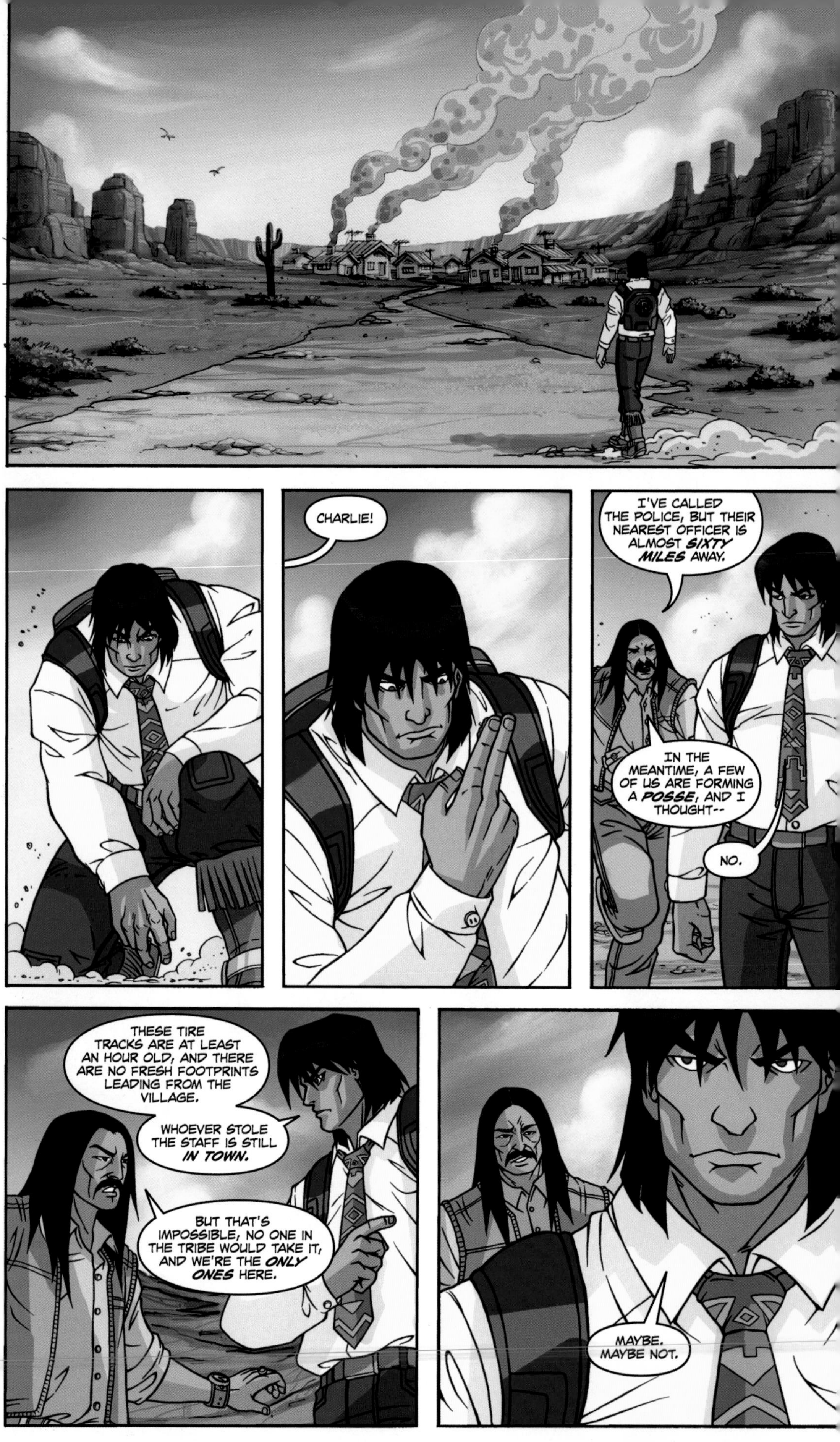
CHARLIE!
I'VE CALLED THE POLICE, BUT THEIR NEAREST OFFICER IS ALMOST SIXTY MILES AWAY.
IN THE MEANTIME, A FEW OF US ARE FORMING A POSSE, AND I THOUGHT--
NO.
THESE TIRE TRACKS ARE AT LEAST AN HOUR OLD, AND THERE ARE NO FRESH FOOTPRINTS LEADING FROM THE VILLAGE.
WHOEVER STOLE THE STAFF IS STILL IN TOWN.
BUT THAT'S IMPOSSIBLE, NO ONE IN THE TRIBE WOULD TAKE IT, AND WE'RE THE ONLY ONES HERE.
MAYBE. MAYBE NOT.

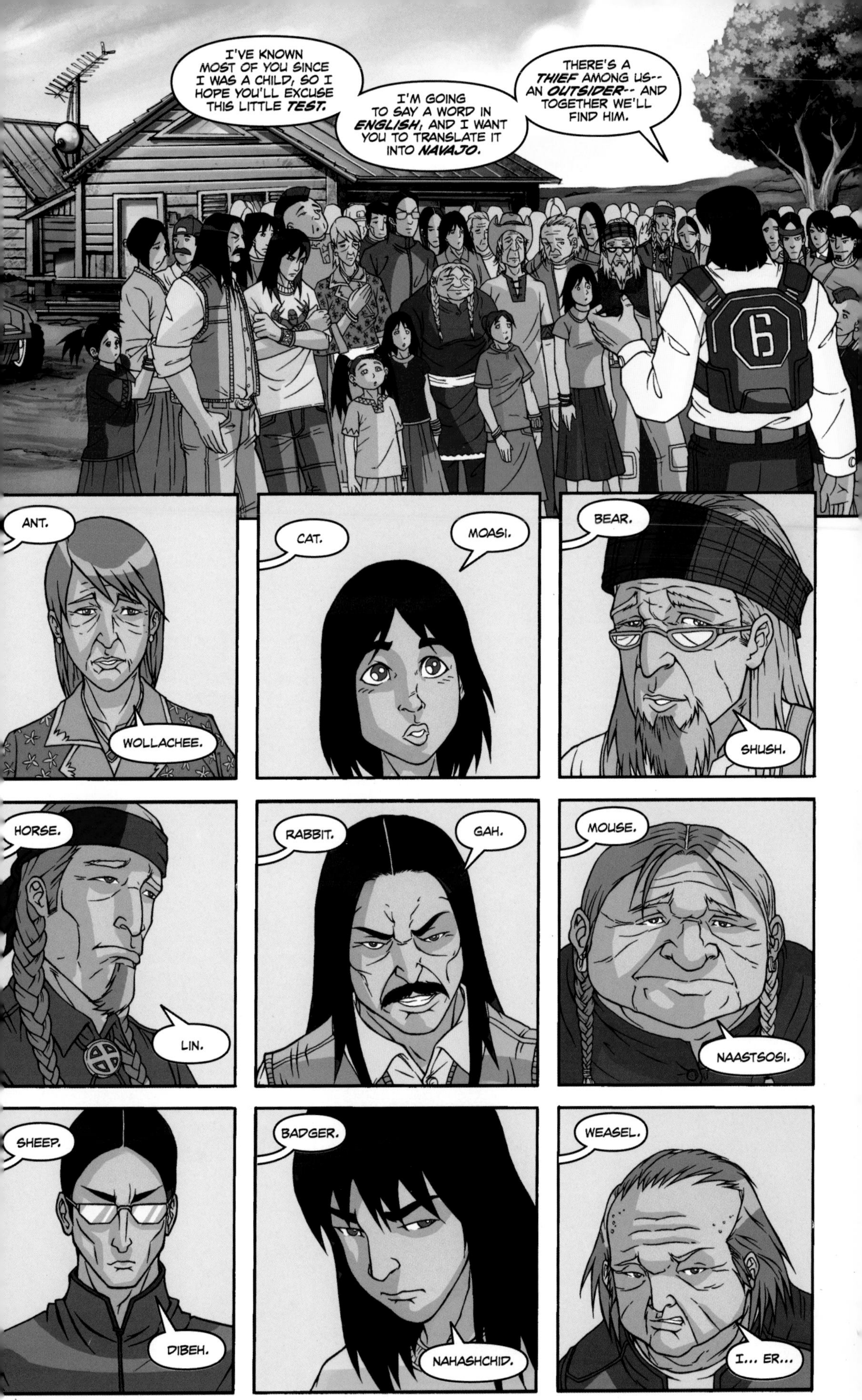
I'VE KNOWN MOST OF YOU SINCE I WAS A CHILD, SO I HOPE YOU'LL EXCUSE THIS LITTLE TEST.
I'M GOING TO SAY A WORD IN ENGLISH, AND I WANT YOU TO TRANSLATE IT INTO NAVAJO.
THERE'S A THIEF AMONG US-- AN OUTSIDER-- AND TOGETHER WE'LL FIND HIM.
ANT.
WOLLACHEE.
CAT.
MOASI.
BEAR.
SHUSH.
HORSE.
LIN.
RABBIT.
GAH.
MOUSE.
NAASTSOSI.
SHEEP.
DIBEH.
BADGER.
NAHASHCHID.
WEASEL.
I... ER...

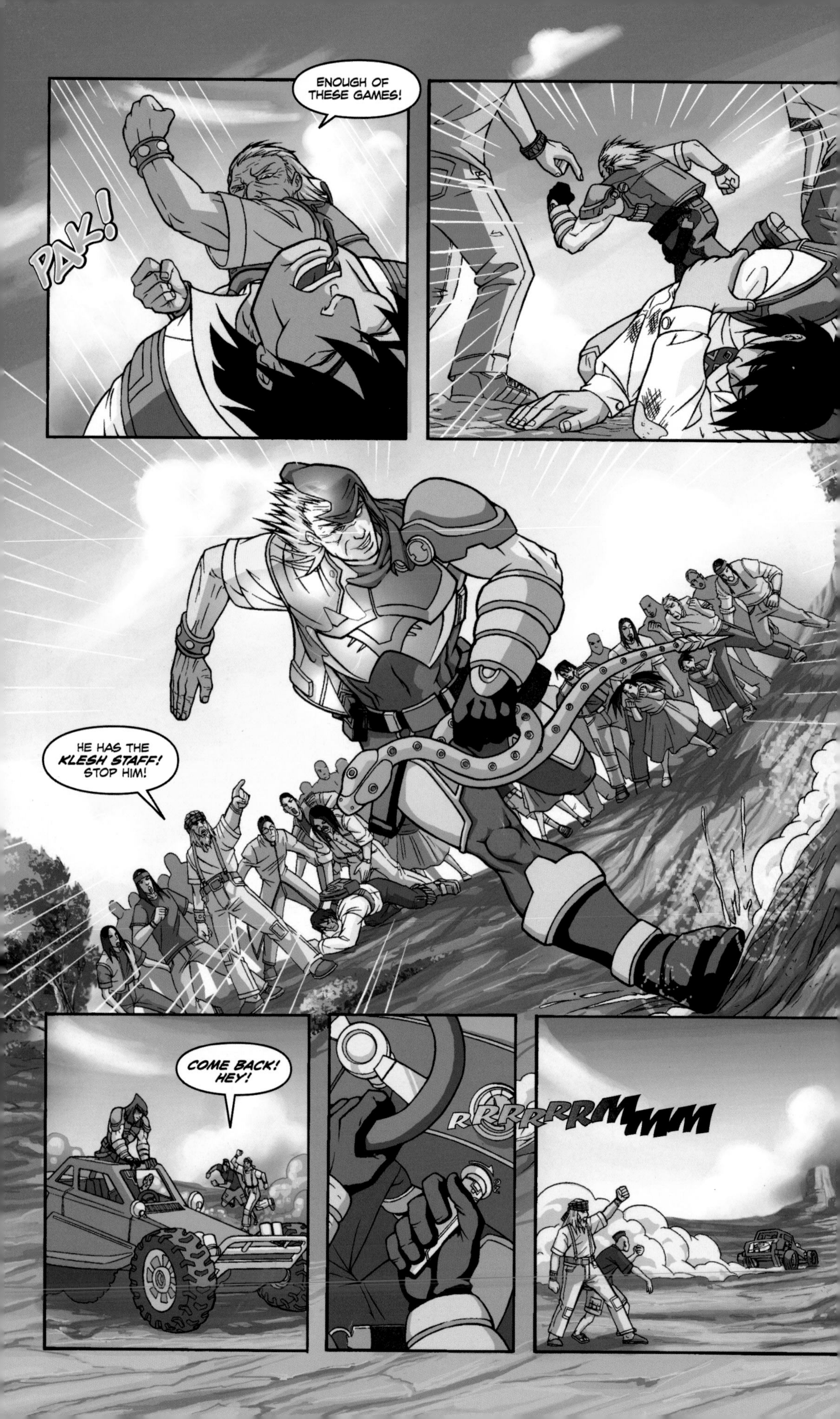
ENOUGH OF THESE GAMES!
PAK!
HE HAS THE KLESH STAFF! STOP HIM!
COME BACK! HEY!
RRRRRRRMMMM

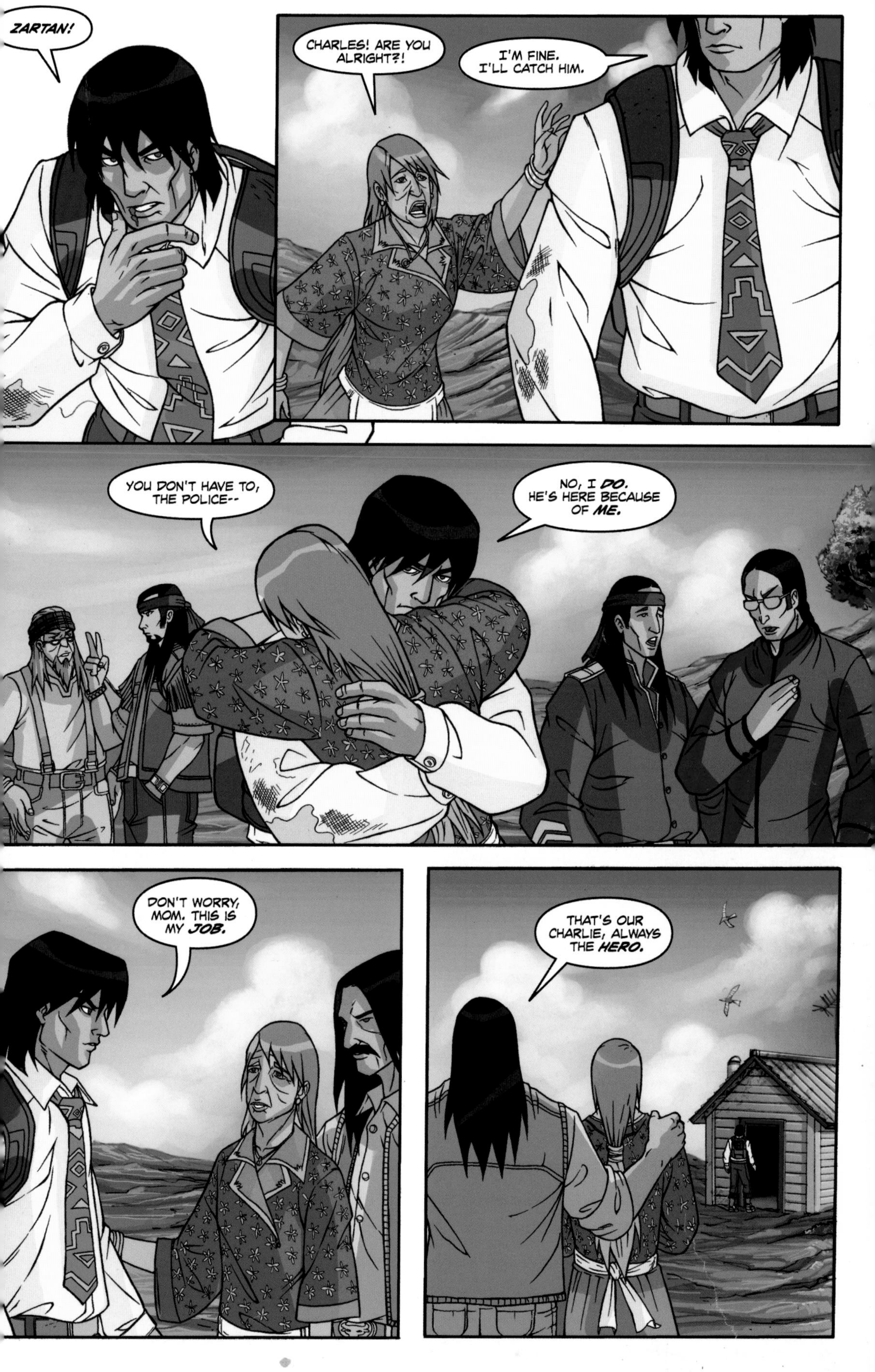
ZARTAN!
CHARLES! ARE YOU ALRIGHT?!
I'M FINE. I'LL CATCH HIM.
YOU DON'T HAVE TO, THE POLICE--
NO, I *DO*. HE'S HERE BECAUSE OF *ME*.
DON'T WORRY, MOM. THIS IS MY *JOB*.
THAT'S OUR CHARLIE, ALWAYS THE *HERO*.

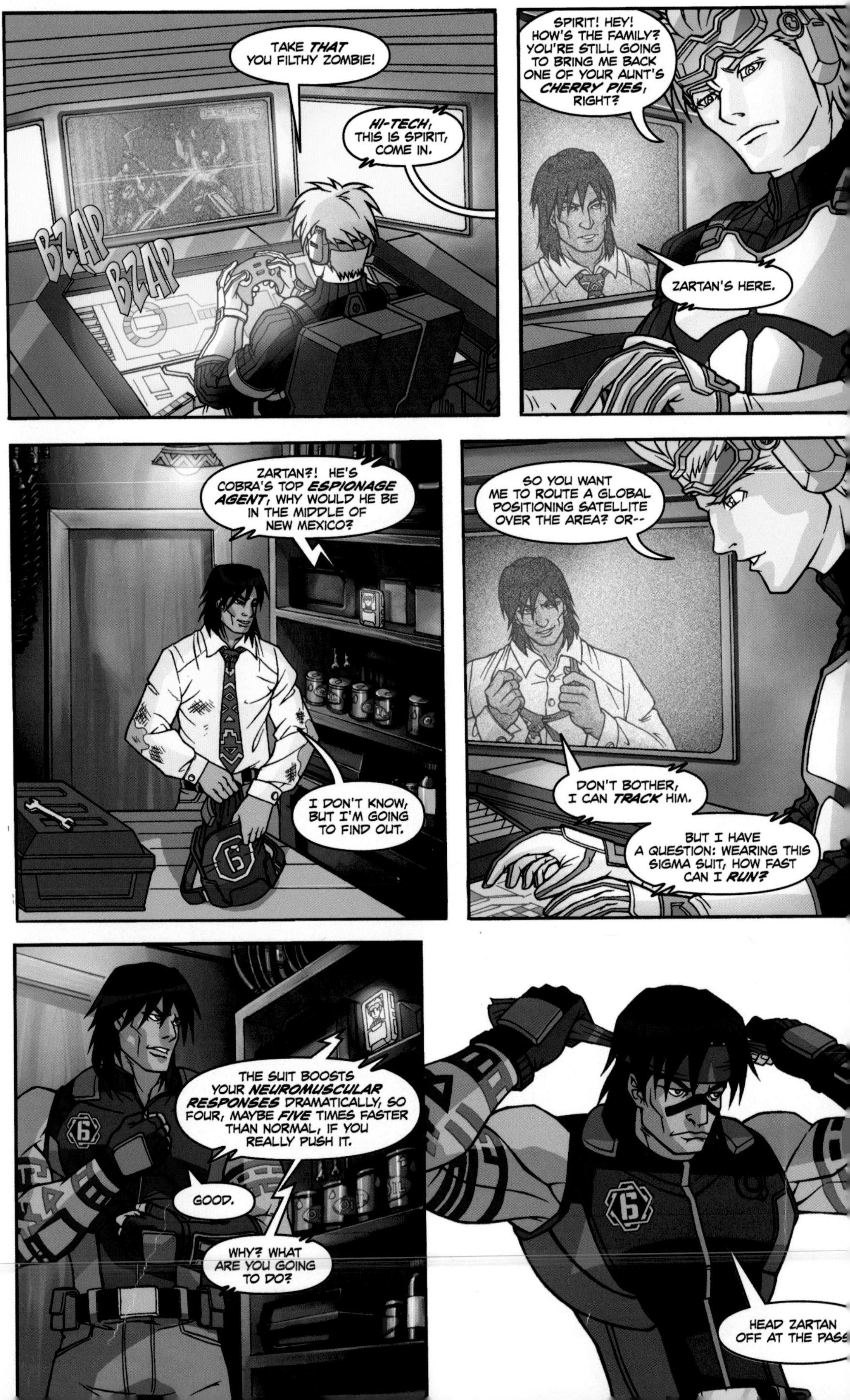
TAKE THAT YOU FILTHY ZOMBIE!
HI-TECH, THIS IS SPIRIT, COME IN.
BZAP BZAP
SPIRIT! HEY! HOW'S THE FAMILY? YOU'RE STILL GOING TO BRING ME BACK ONE OF YOUR AUNT'S CHERRY PIES, RIGHT?
ZARTAN'S HERE.
ZARTAN?! HE'S COBRA'S TOP ESPIONAGE AGENT, WHY WOULD HE BE IN THE MIDDLE OF NEW MEXICO?
I DON'T KNOW, BUT I'M GOING TO FIND OUT.
SO YOU WANT ME TO ROUTE A GLOBAL POSITIONING SATELLITE OVER THE AREA? OR--
DON'T BOTHER, I CAN TRACK HIM.
BUT I HAVE A QUESTION: WEARING THIS SIGMA SUIT, HOW FAST CAN I RUN?
THE SUIT BOOSTS YOUR NEUROMUSCULAR RESPONSES DRAMATICALLY, SO FOUR, MAYBE FIVE TIMES FASTER THAN NORMAL, IF YOU REALLY PUSH IT.
GOOD.
WHY? WHAT ARE YOU GOING TO DO?
HEAD ZARTAN OFF AT THE PASS

THMMMMMMM

WOW...

Kasawaki

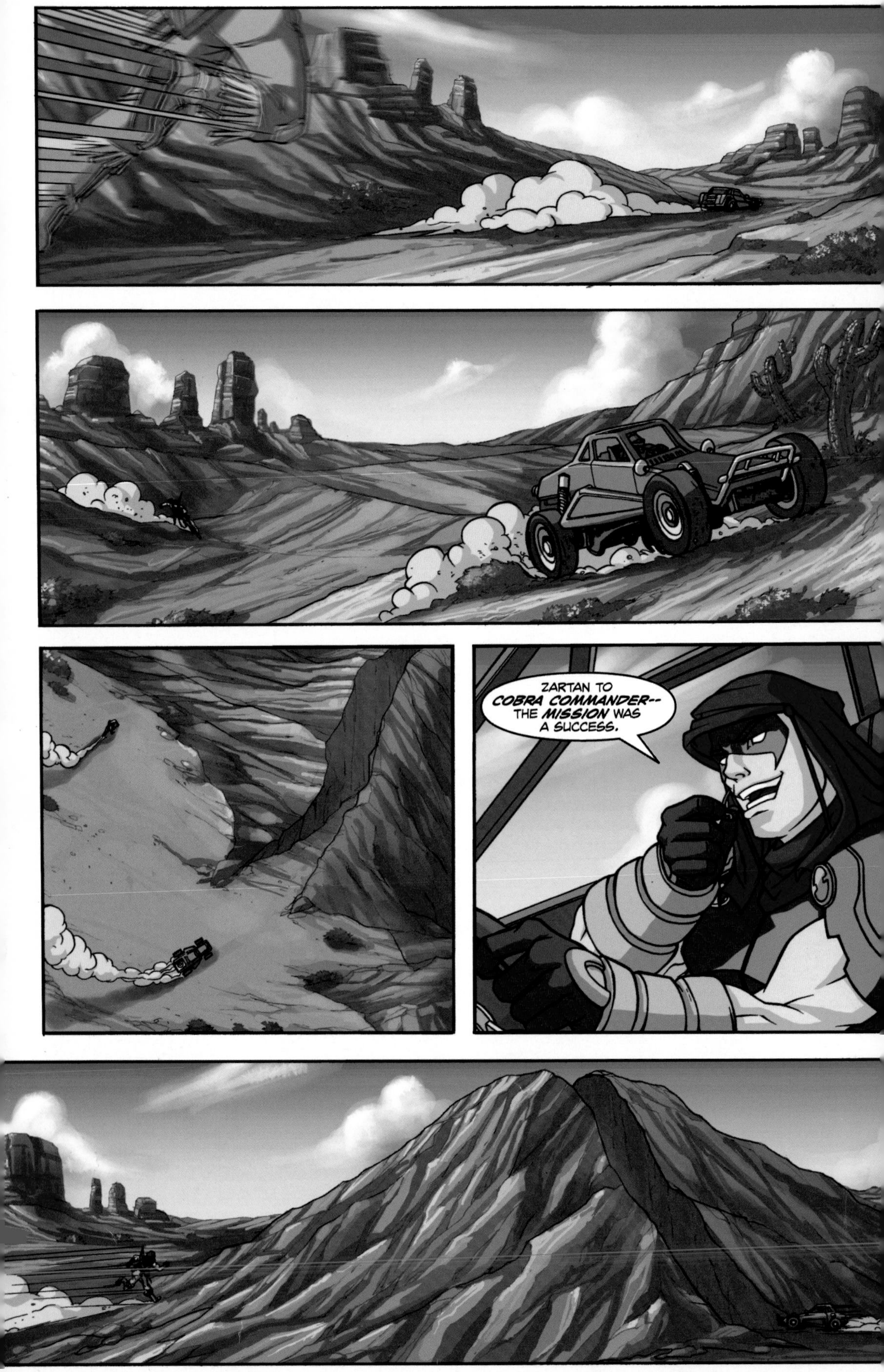
ZARTAN TO
COBRA COMMANDER--
THE MISSION WAS
A SUCCESS.

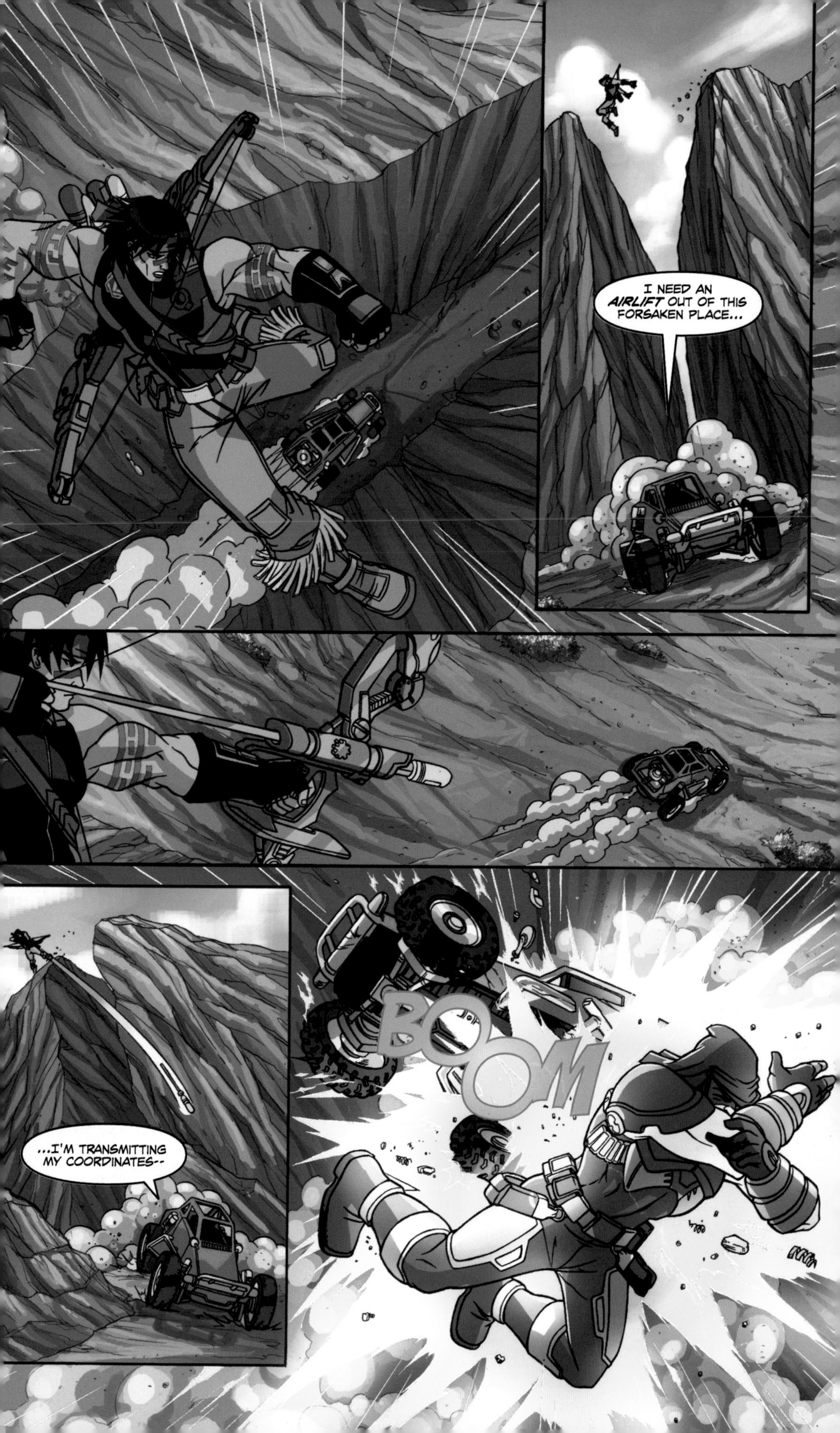
I NEED AN AIRLIFT OUT OF THIS FORSAKEN PLACE...
...I'M TRANSMITTING MY COORDINATES--
BOOOM

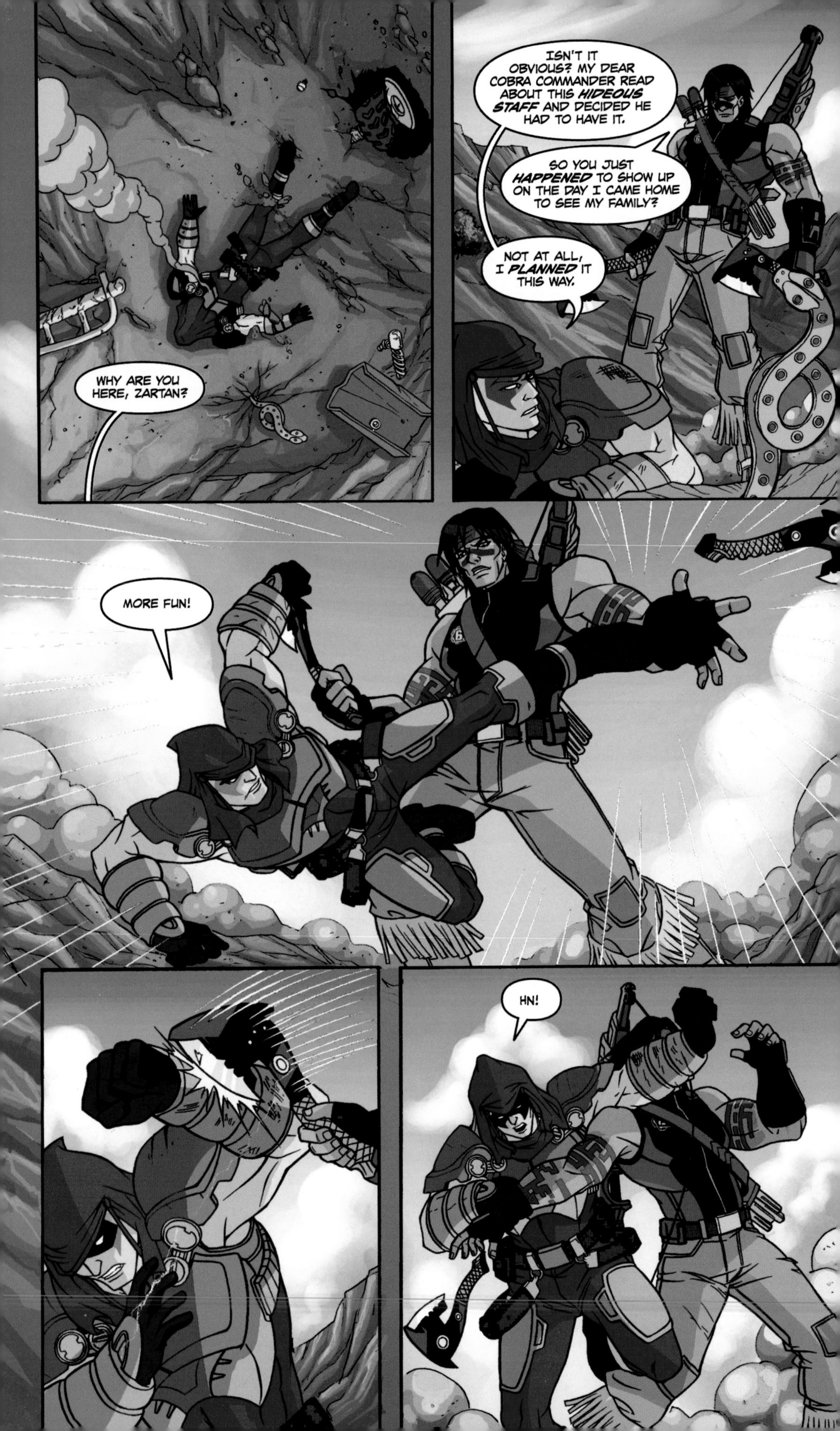
WHY ARE YOU HERE, ZARTAN?
ISN'T IT OBVIOUS? MY DEAR COBRA COMMANDER READ ABOUT THIS HIDEOUS STAFF AND DECIDED HE HAD TO HAVE IT.
SO YOU JUST HAPPENED TO SHOW UP ON THE DAY I CAME HOME TO SEE MY FAMILY?
NOT AT ALL, I PLANNED IT THIS WAY.
MORE FUN!
HN!

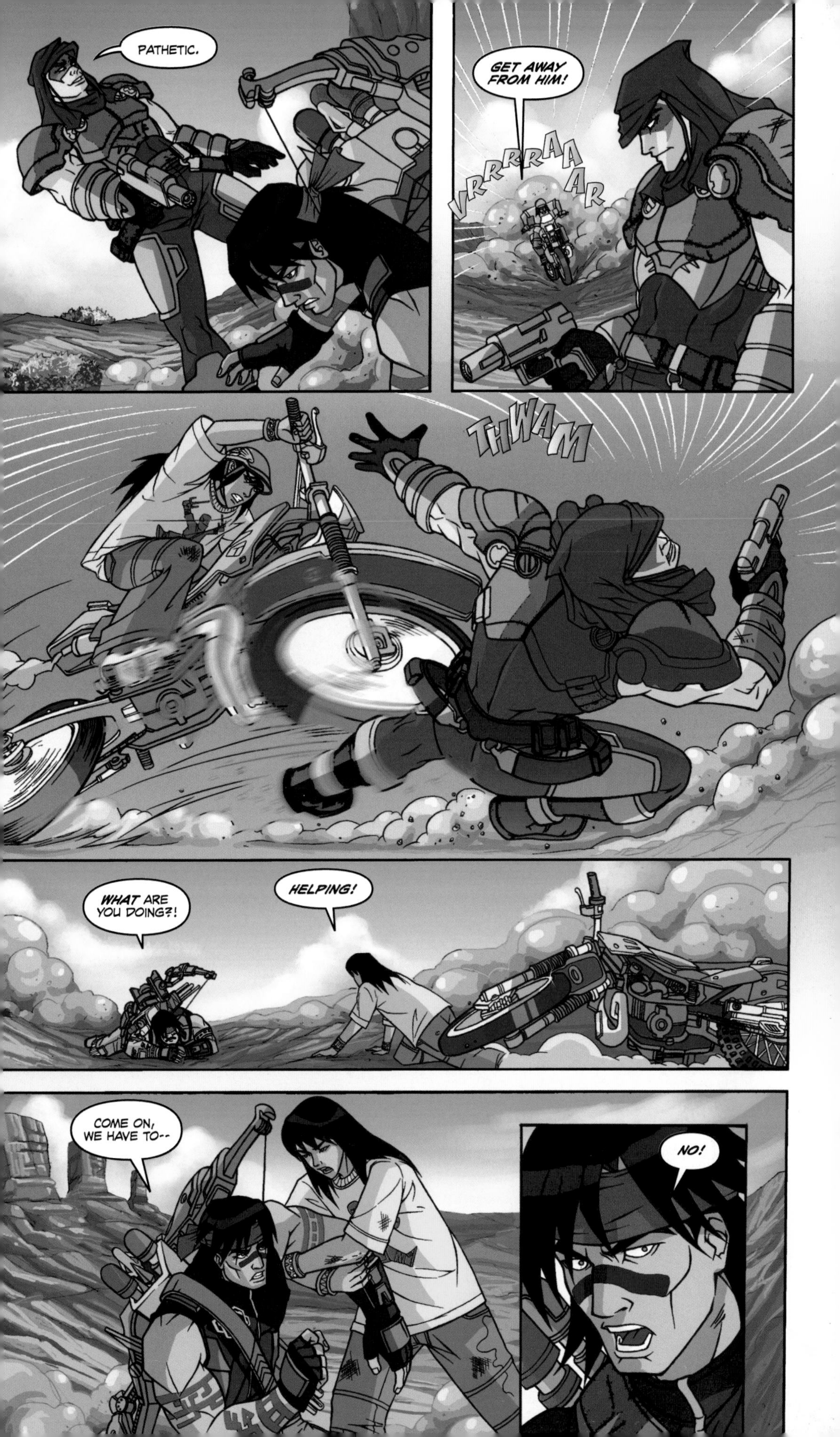
PATHETIC.
GET AWAY FROM HIM!
VRRRRAAAAR
THWAM
WHAT ARE YOU DOING?!
HELPING!
COME ON, WE HAVE TO--
NO!

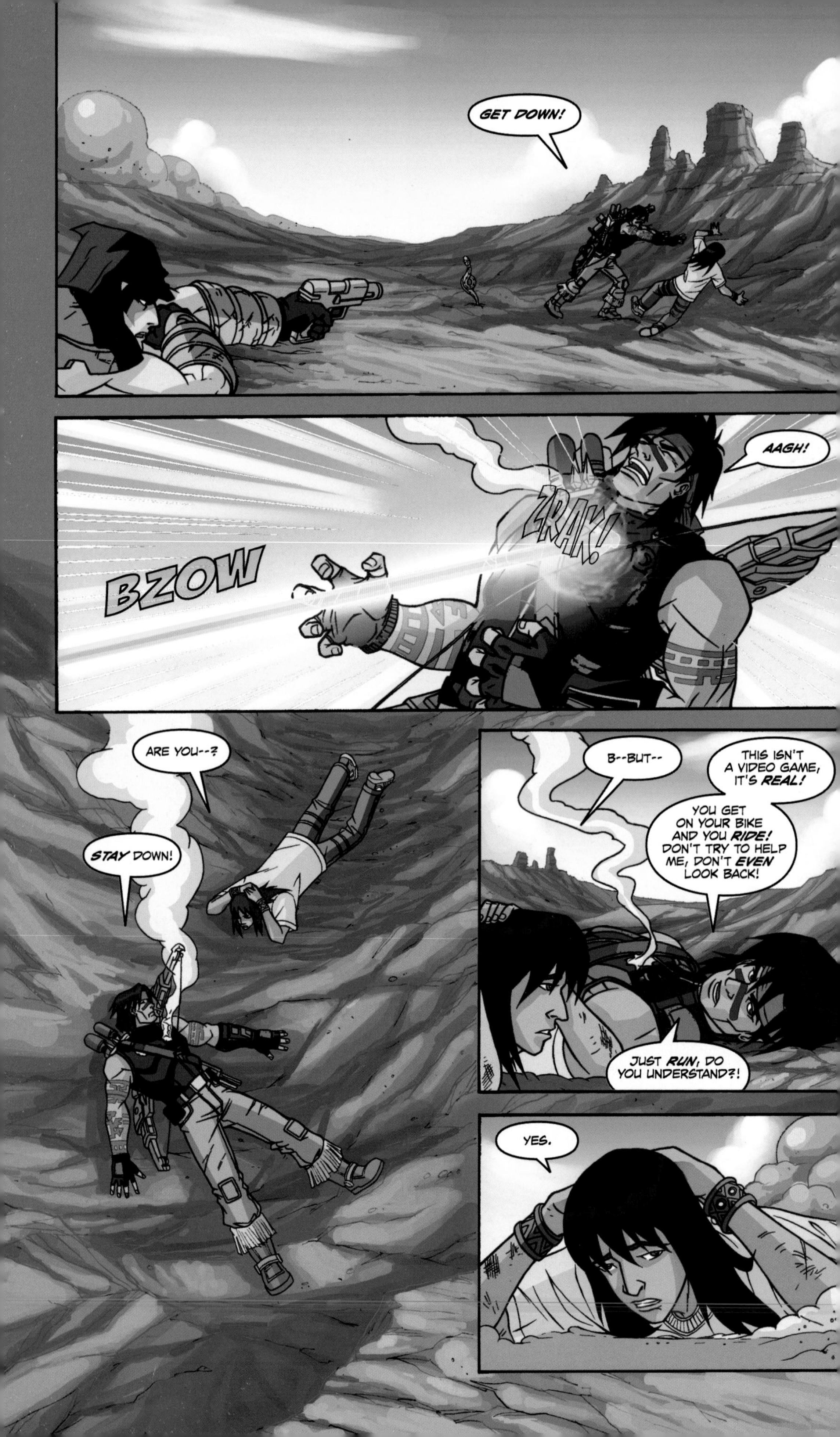
GET DOWN!
AAGH!
ZRAK!
BZOW
ARE YOU--?
STAY DOWN!
B--BUT--
THIS ISN'T A VIDEO GAME, IT'S REAL!
YOU GET ON YOUR BIKE AND YOU RIDE! DON'T TRY TO HELP ME, DON'T EVEN LOOK BACK!
JUST RUN, DO YOU UNDERSTAND?!
YES.

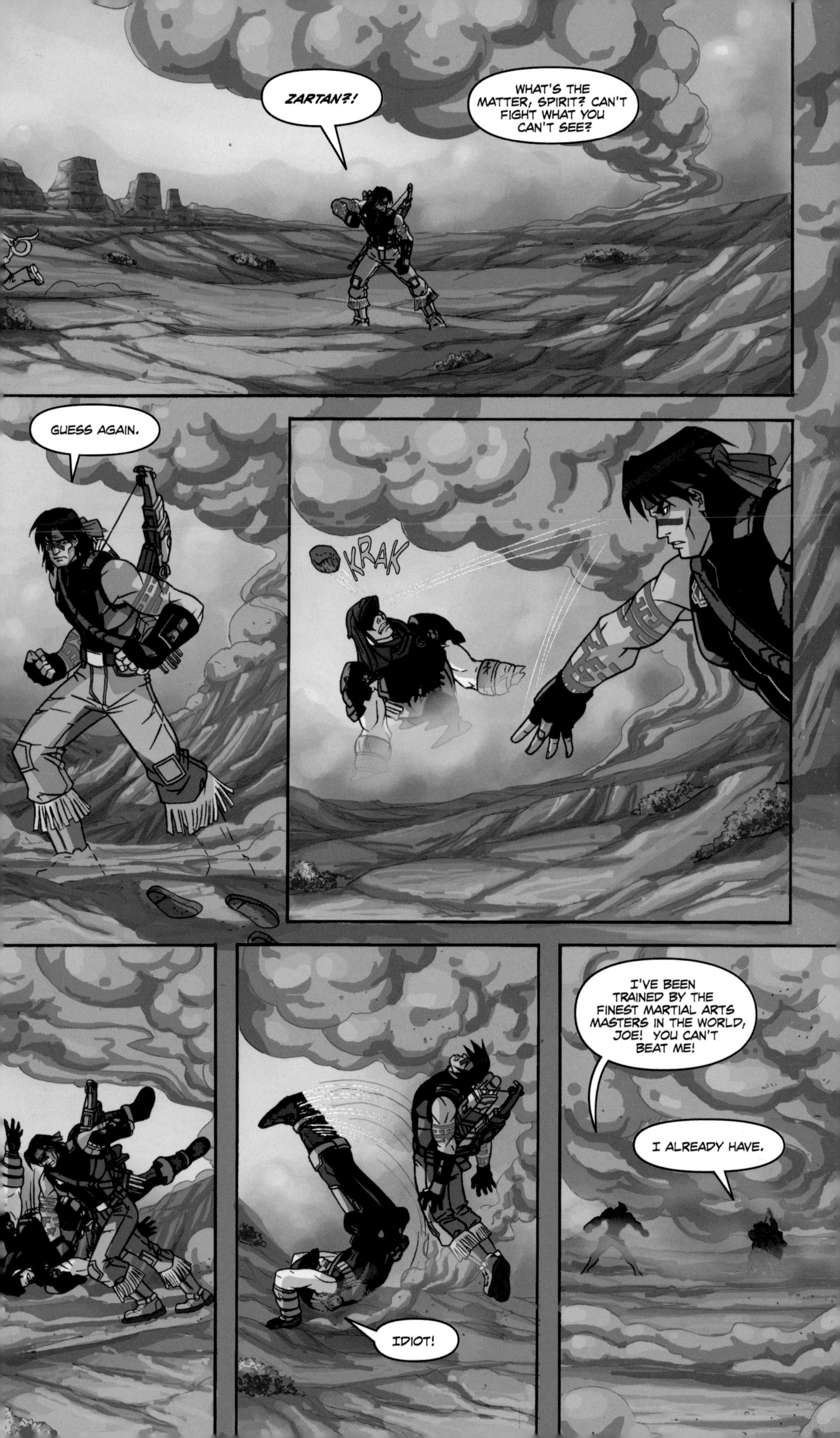
ZARTAN?!
WHAT'S THE MATTER, SPIRIT? CAN'T FIGHT WHAT YOU CAN'T SEE?
GUESS AGAIN.
KRAK
I'VE BEEN TRAINED BY THE FINEST MARTIAL ARTS MASTERS IN THE WORLD, JOE! YOU CAN'T BEAT ME!
IDIOT!
I ALREADY HAVE.

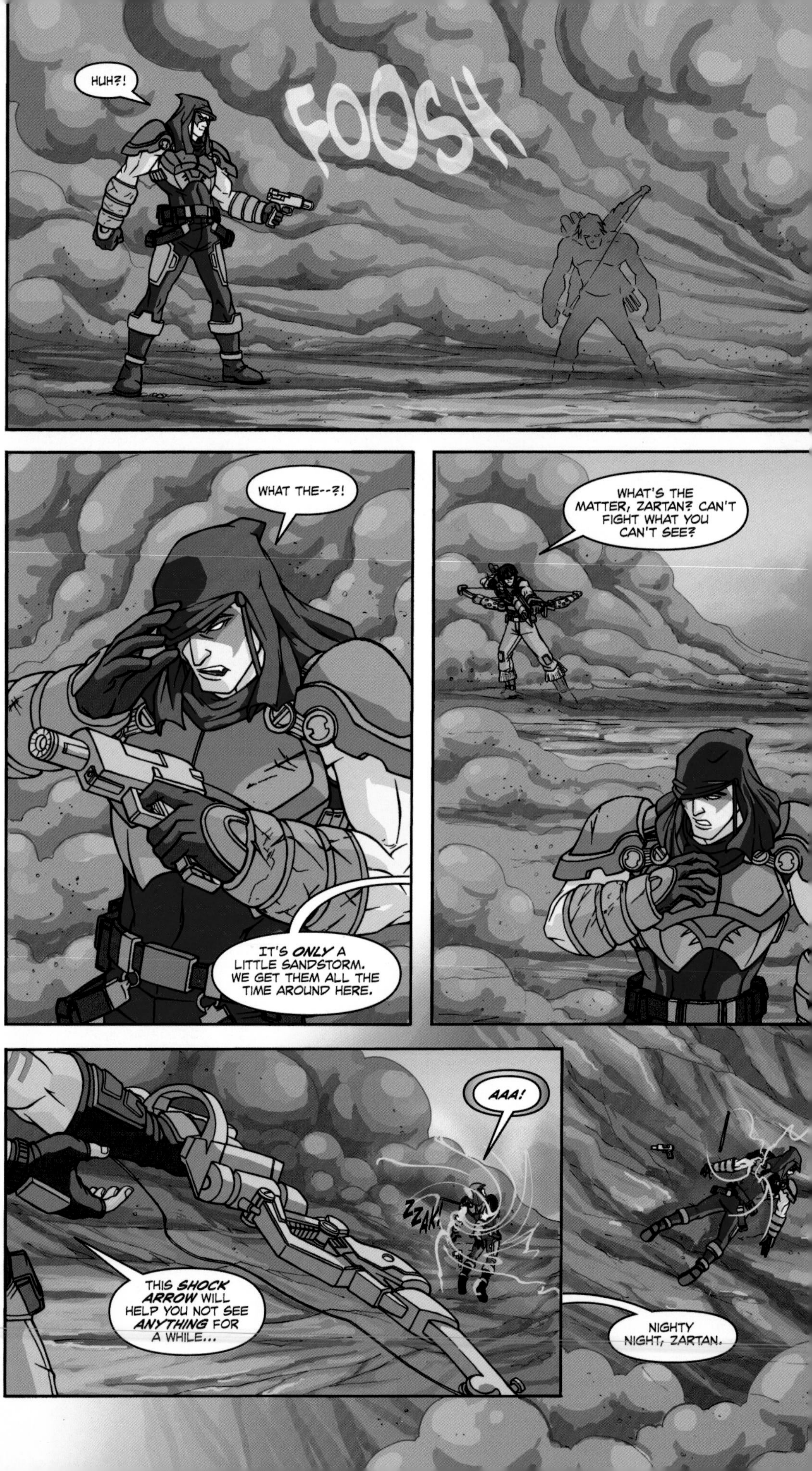
HUH?!
FOOSH
WHAT THE--?!
IT'S *ONLY* A LITTLE SANDSTORM. WE GET THEM ALL THE TIME AROUND HERE.
WHAT'S THE MATTER, ZARTAN? CAN'T FIGHT WHAT YOU CAN'T SEE?
AAA!
ZZAK!
THIS ***SHOCK ARROW*** WILL HELP YOU NOT SEE ***ANYTHING*** FOR A WHILE...
NIGHTY NIGHT, ZARTAN.

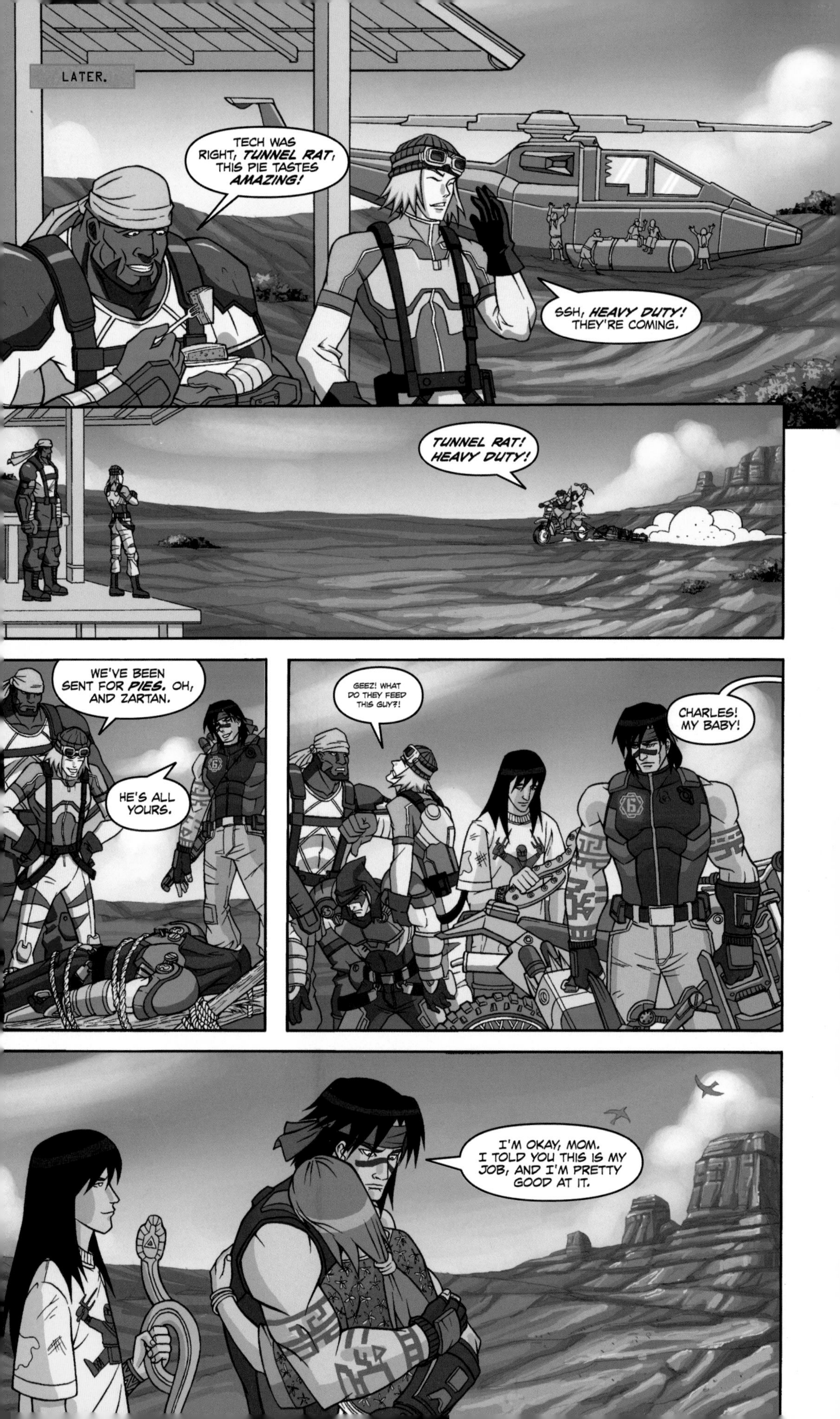
LATER.
TECH WAS RIGHT, TUNNEL RAT, THIS PIE TASTES AMAZING!
SSH, HEAVY DUTY! THEY'RE COMING.
TUNNEL RAT! HEAVY DUTY!
WE'VE BEEN SENT FOR PIES. OH, AND ZARTAN.
HE'S ALL YOURS.
GEEZ! WHAT DO THEY FEED THIS GUY?!
CHARLES! MY BABY!
I'M OKAY, MOM. I TOLD YOU THIS IS MY JOB, AND I'M PRETTY GOOD AT IT.

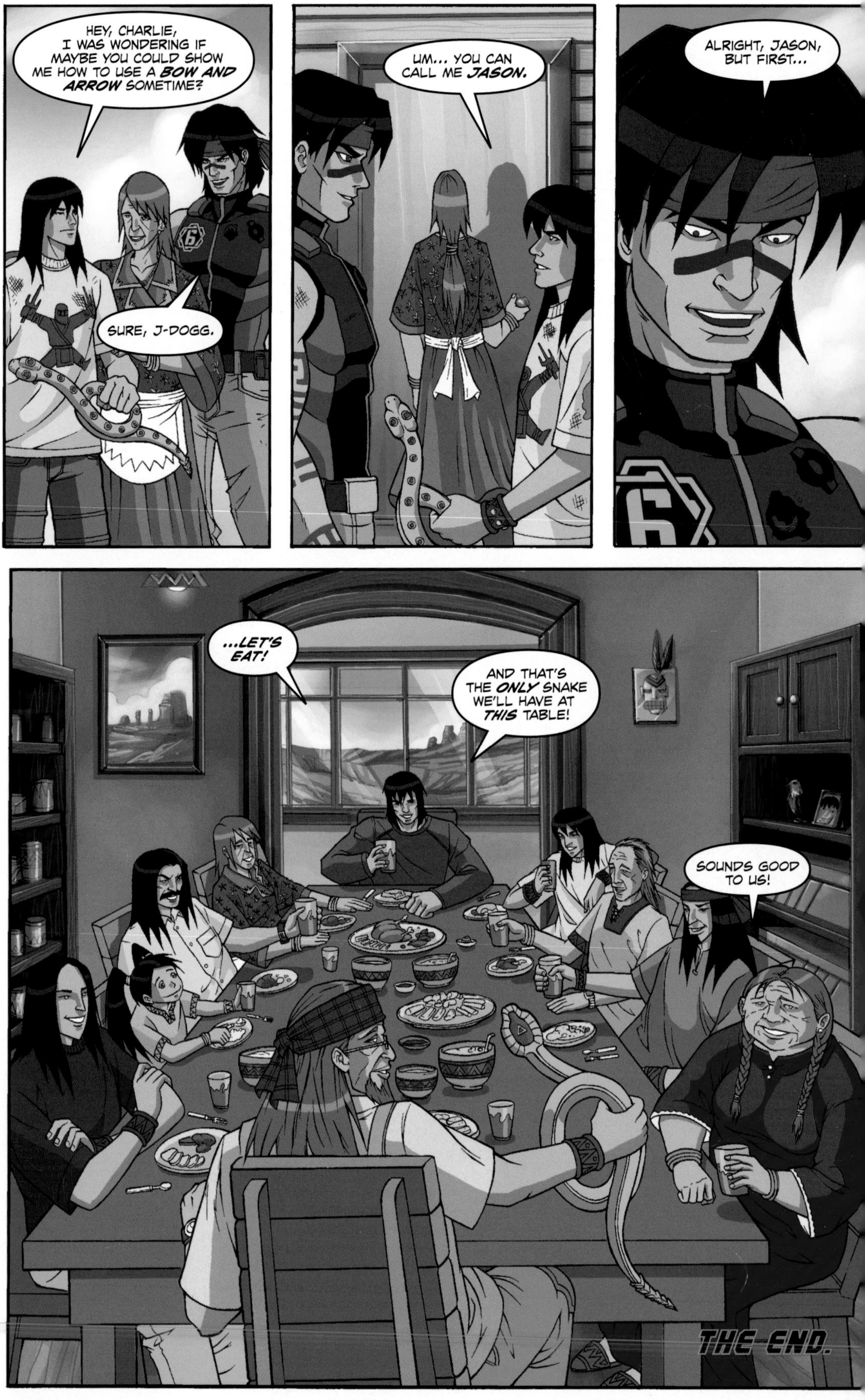
HEY, CHARLIE, I WAS WONDERING IF MAYBE YOU COULD SHOW ME HOW TO USE A BOW AND ARROW SOMETIME?
SURE, J-DOGG.
UM... YOU CAN CALL ME JASON.
ALRIGHT, JASON, BUT FIRST...
...LET'S EAT!
AND THAT'S THE ONLY SNAKE WE'LL HAVE AT THIS TABLE!
SOUNDS GOOD TO US!
THE END.